ANIMORPHS
THE INVASION

ORPHS
THE INVASION

K.A. APPLEGATE & **MICHAEL GRANT**
A GRAPHIC NOVEL BY **CHRIS GRINE**

graphix
An Imprint of

■SCHOLASTIC

Text copyright © 2020 by Katherine Applegate
Art copyright © 2020 by Chris Grine

Library of Congress Control Number Available

ISBN 978-1-338-22648-5 (hardcover)
ISBN 978-1-338-53809-0 (paperback)

10 9 8 7 6 5 4 3 2 1   20 21 22 23 24

Printed in China   62
First edition, October 2020
Edited by Zack Clark
Book design by Phil Falco
Publisher: David Saylor

For Ani-fans everywhere.
You're the best fandom ever.
–KAA & MR

For Robyn, who could clearly
see what she was getting into but
married me anyway
–CG

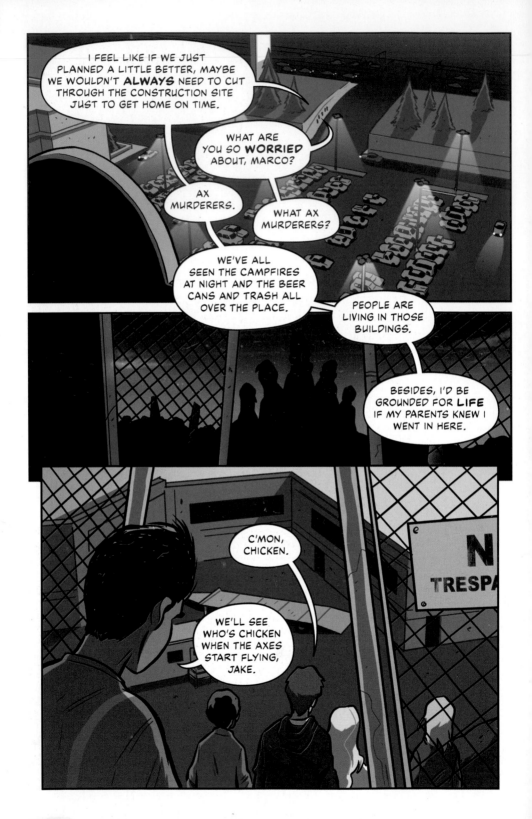

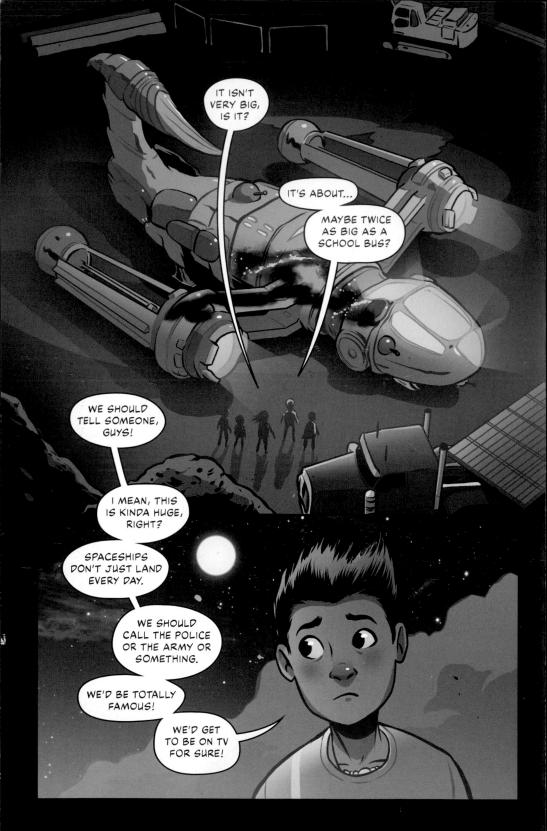

16

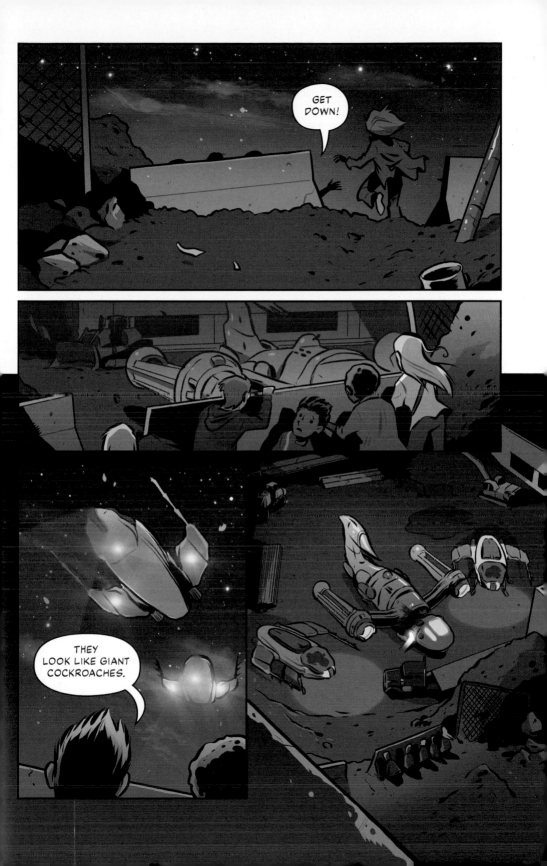

FOOMMMMMMMM

THOSE CONSTRUCTION GUYS AREN'T GONNA BE HAPPY ABOUT THAT.

THE DOORS ARE OPENING, GUYS.

WE NEED TO *GO!*

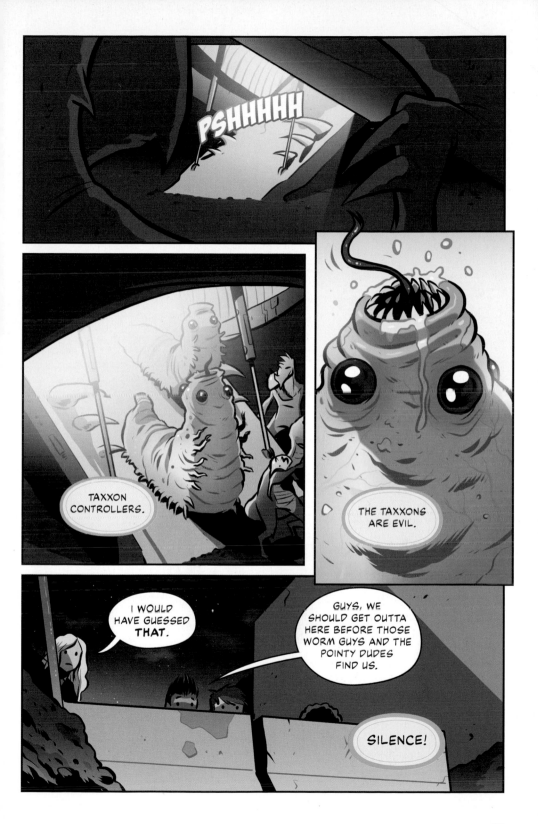

45

55

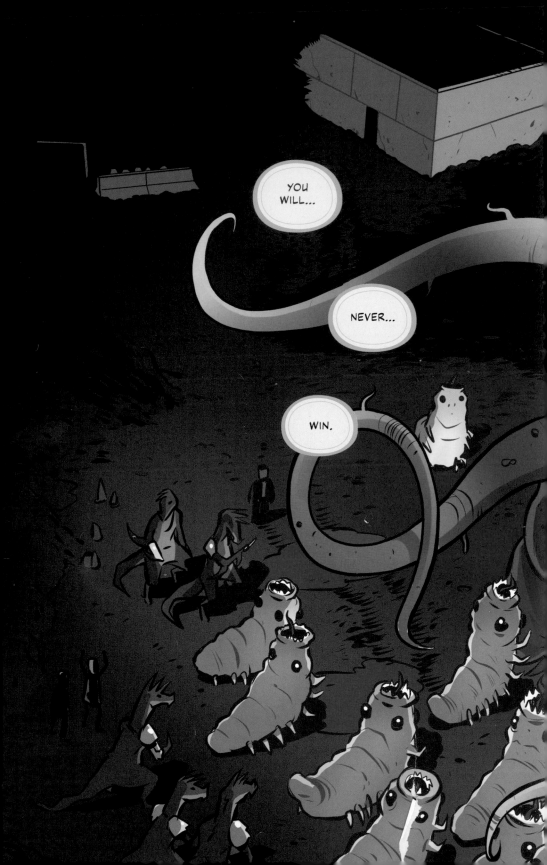

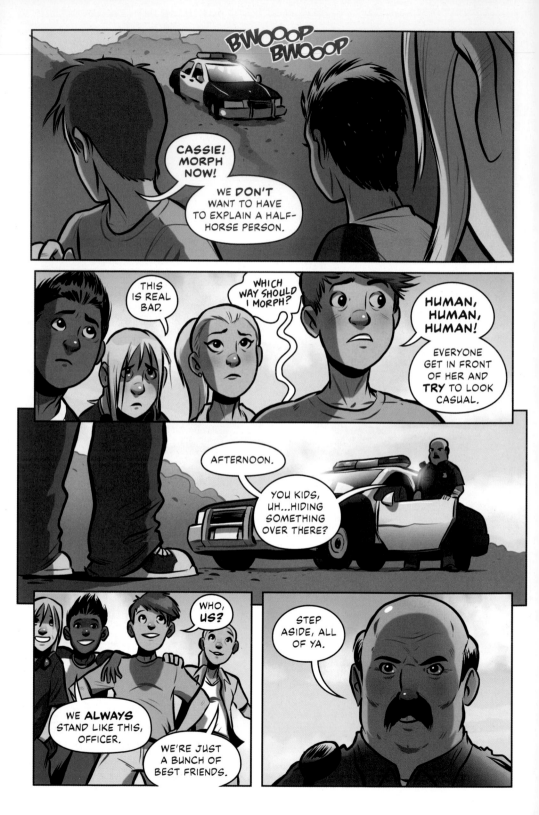

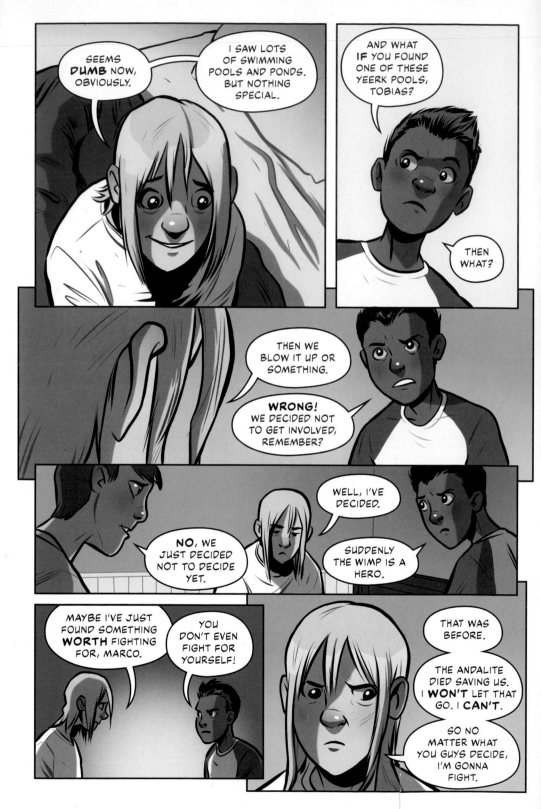

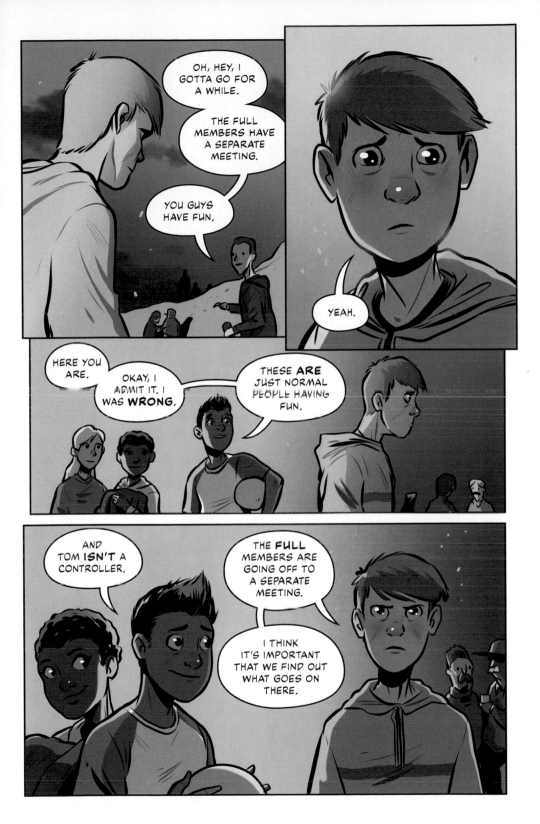

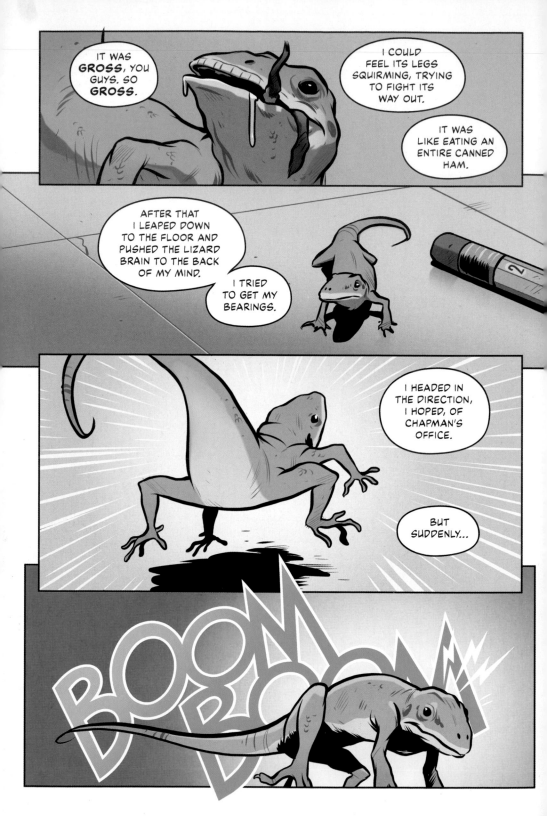

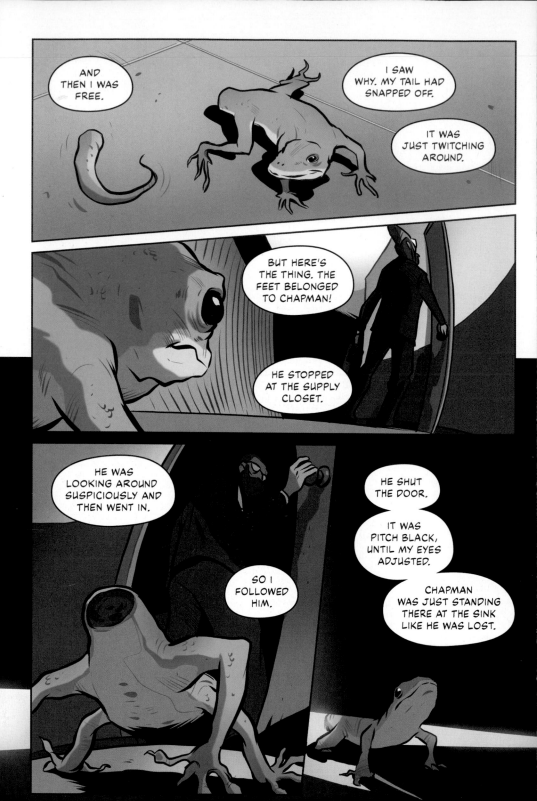

140

157

THAT'S WEIRD. THERE'S NO GATE THAT...

AAAGGHHH!!

GULP

SLAM

WRONG DOOR!

DOOR NUMBER TWO!

169

199

205

207

214

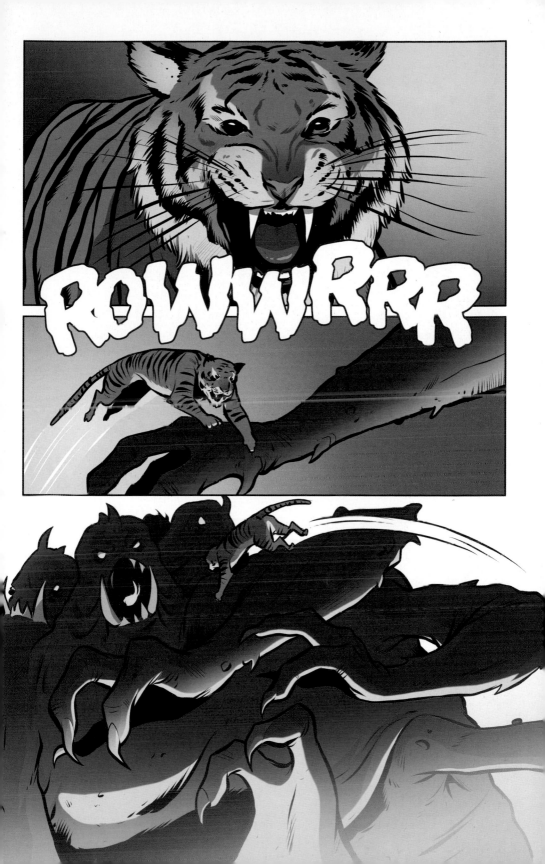

K.A. APPLEGATE is the married writing team Katherine Applegate and Michael Grant. Their Animorphs™ series has sold millions of copies worldwide and alerted the world to the presence of the Yeerks. Katherine is also the author of the Endling series and the Newbery Medal–winning *The One and Only Ivan*. Michael is also the author of the Front Lines and Gone series.

CHRIS GRINE is the creator of Chickenhare and *Time Shifters*. He's been making up stories since he was a kid, and not just to get out of trouble with his parents. Nowadays, Chris spends most of his time writing and illustrating books, drinking lots of coffee, and sleeping as little as possible. He spends his free time with his wife, playing with his kids, watching movies, and collecting action figures (but only the bad guys).

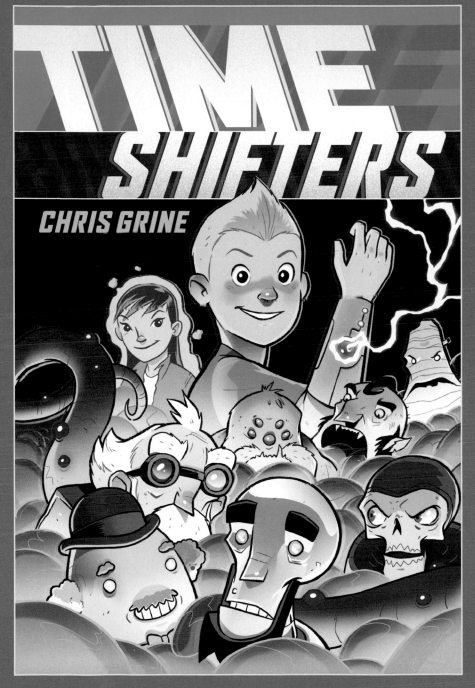

TO BE CONTINUED . . .

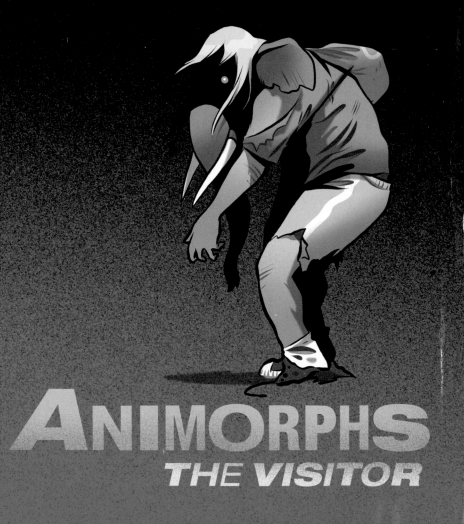

ANIMORPHS
THE VISITOR